THE WIN WITHIN

CHRISTON "THE TRUTH" JONES

WRITTEN BY
CHRISTON JONES

ILLUSTRATED BY
MARCUS WILLIAMS

ISBN: 978-1534884502
Library of Congress Control Number: 2015955698
Printed in the United States of America

⊗ This paper meets the requirements of
ANSI/NISO Z39.48-1992 (Permanence of Paper)

Dedication

I would like to dedicate The Win Within to the coaching staff at Pinellas Park Thunderbirds, Clearwater Titians, Offense Defense Camp, and Ultimate Stomping Ground. To my mentors Tony Dungy, Peyton Manning, Cam Newton Ray Lewis, Marshawn Lynch, Eric Thomas, and Stuart Scott. I want to express my deepest gratitude for opening my eyes to new level of work ethic and professionalism.

Christon stood in line to sign up for the
school's Pee Wee football team. The sweat
dripped down the back of his neck and side
of his face. "Man, Miami's hot. It's sand-hopping,
nose-drippin' hot." The boy behind him tapped
Christon's shoulder. "Hey, I'm Pete. You're new
here. Where ya from?"

"I'm Christon. We came from Fort Knox, Kentucky.
My parents are in the Army."

"Way cool," said Pete. "Ever play football before?"
An easy smile crept up on Christon's face.
"I sure did. My team had two undefeated flag
football seasons. This is my first tackle
team though."

"I never played before," said Pete. "Maybe, you
can give me some tips."

"NEXT," called the coach.

Christon flung his book bag over his shoulder.

"Sure." He went to the desk and signed up.

Pete ran to Christon on the field. "First practice. You ready?"

"Hey, Pete. I'm always ready for football. I've dreamed of being the number one running back and most feared defensive linebacker since I was five. I'm hoping that dream comes true here."

"Okay, boys. Line up." A voice boomed from behind the boys. "For you who don't know me yet, I'm Coach Tony."

"Whoa! He's big," said Pete. "He's gotta be way over 6 feet and over 200 pounds. The other guys said he's a hard-nosed, in-your-face, detail obsessed New Yorker. He won four straight Super Bowl titles. Everyone calls him Face, because he gets right up in everyone's face."

Christon shook his head.

"Man, you're full of information."

Christon hit the dirt hard. He got up and brushed himself off.

"You alright?" said Pete.

"Yeah. The first week is the hardest. The coaches are checking us rookies out. They need to know what we're made of and if we have any talent. They want to see how we stack up to the veteran players." Pete slapped Christon on the back.

"But, this is only the first practice. Do they have to be so hard on us?"

"Listen up." Coach always sounded like he was yelling. "We have unfinished business here. We have one goal and one mission, to win the Super Bowl and bring home our trophy."

"Hey Pete," whispered Christon, "this is how I imagined football would be in the Sunshine state. It's football paradise."

The next day in school, Christon and Pete sat eating lunch and reading the football bulletin. "Check this out," said Pete. "The Quarterback, Paul Manning, #18, is 9 years old, 55 inches, and weighs 65 pounds. They call him The Noodle. Everyone says he's a clean cut kid who keeps calm and knows how to take control of the field."

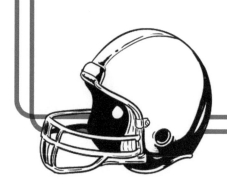

"Cool. Check out the Running Back, Mike Lynch, #24. He's 8, 50 inches tall, and weighs 60 pounds. They call him The Juke. It says he's fast and strong. I heard the Coach say he jukes all the linebackers with his spin moves. And, he blocks the defensive backs with a super stiff arm."

Christon looked over Pete's shoulder. "What about the Defensive End, Roy Lewis, #52."
"It says he's 8 years old, 51 inches tall, and weighs 98 pounds. CREEPS, I wouldn't want to be on the other end of his tackle." Pete crunched his face up and put his arms over his head. Christon shook his head. "Okay, stop being dramatic. What's the rest of his stats?"
"It says he's big and he's strong. They call him The Ox. Did you see him on the field yesterday? It looks like he's playing against preschoolers." The bell rang and Christon picked up his tray. "Looks like we have a pretty good team. See you at practice."

"Man, I'm so happy I'm on this team," said Christon. Pete shrugged. "I'll let you know at the end of the week."

The coach gathered the team. "Listen up. You'll train like me. You'll think like me. And, you'll act like me. Heck, some of you jokers will even start to look like me."

Coach walked around the team, eyeing the boys up. "We train hard, every day for two hours, except Sundays. Remember, we train hard, so when it's game time, it's easy. Our motto is, One Dream, One Team."

"I love this guy," said Christon.

The coach wasn't kidding. The training was brutal.

"Oh, sorry," said Sam.

"What happened," said Pete. Christon shook his head. "Awe, he's just being a jerk. He keeps shoving me after the plays. Some of the other guys are tripping me and shoving me too." Christon took his helmet off. "Last week I was living my dream. This week it's more like a nightmare. I think these guys are bullying me." Pete put his hand on Christon's shoulder.

"I know. They're doing it to me and a couple of other rookies. But, nowhere near as bad as they are to you."

"Yeah. Being a rookie is tough enough. We have to learn the new plays. And, practice two hours a day in sweat-dripping heat. These guys have to make it worse." Christon's shoulders slumped on his walk home. His head hung low. His book bag felt heavier than usual.

The next day at practice, Christon took his three-point stance. He screwed his face into the fiercest look he could. He concentrated on the play, ready to move fast. Up from behind him, Joe, the Safety, pushed his foot into the back of Christon's knee. Down Christon went.

"Hey!" yelled Pete. He ran to his friend and helped him up. "You okay?"

Christon shook his head. "Yeah, I'm good. I didn't really get hurt. But, so much for my fierce stance."

A few of the veteran players walked past Christon and laughed.

A couple of days later, at practice, the team just finished a play. Luke, the Fullback, ran up to Christon and shoved him with all his might. Christon went flying and landed hard. He lay on the ground looking at the sky. "What am I doing here?"

Pete and some other teammates raced to Christon. "Buddy, we saw that. Can you get up?" said Pete. Christon wobbled to his feet.

"Whoa. I felt my brain shake with that hit. Did the coach see it?"

Pete grabbed Christon's arm to help steady him. "I don't think so. Coach is at the other end of the field."

"This is crazy," said Christon. "I know these guys are tough and aggressive like Coach. They're NO FEAR football players. But, hey, I'm their teammate. Enough is enough."

Pete walked Christon to the lockers. "I'm sorry this is happening. Why don't you tell someone?"

"You know, I'm the new kid in the school. A new kid on the football team. And, I'm being bullied by my own teammates. It stinks. I can't remember ever feeling this bad."

Christon threw his helmet in his locker and sat on the bench. He put his head in his hands. "How is this happening? In Kentucky I was the superstar player. Now, I'm being bullied. And, being bullied on the football field of all places."

The boys changed and left the locker. "Want me to come over your house for a while?" said Pete.

"No. I'll be fine. I'll see you tomorrow. Thanks, though."

Christon took the long way home. He didn't want to see anyone, not even his parents.

It's crazy, the one place I always felt happy and at peace was on the football field. It was my little piece of heaven, my paradise. The place where I belonged. Do I talk to the coach or my parents? But, if I tell an adult, the bullying could get worse. I have a problem, a big problem.

"Hi, Champ. You're late." Mom met Christon at the door. Christon walked past his mom. "Sorry. Just took the long way home."

"You know," said Mom, "I've noticed that you're not your super-fun self lately. You're not smiling or joking around like you usually do. What's going on?"

Christon tightened his lips. His body stiffened. Then like a flood, it gushed out, "The kids on my team are bullying me. They trip me and shove me after the plays are over. It's really bothering me. I don't know what to do."

Mom put her arm around Christon. "Why didn't you tell me sooner? You know two heads are always better than one. Let's figure out how you can fix this."

Mom took Christon's Bible from his bookshelf. She turned to Deuteronomy 31:6 and read, "Be strong and courageous. Do not be afraid of them, for the Lord your God goes with you; he will never leave you alone."

"Son, you're strong. You're smart and talented. Try to remember that. Be true to yourself. Don't be afraid of your teammates. Lord your God goes with you. He'll always be with you. Just look within yourself."

"Thanks for the reminder, Mom. I know all that stuff. I have to remember to apply it." Christon lay in bed that night, calm and relaxed. Right before he closed his eyes, he heard, "Everything you need to win is within you."

The next day during school, Christon whispered a poem he learned when he was little. He said it over and over:

I will always place the Team first.

I will never accept defeat.

I will never quit.

I will leave it all on the field.

After school, Christon met Pete on the field. It was another rough practice. When the whistle blew for the last play, Sam pushed Christon.

"Ha, ha. Good one." Christon slapped Sam on the back. When he turned to walk away, Joe shoved him into the practice dummy."

"That's pretty funny." Christon slapped Joe on the back. Joe and Sam looked at Christon, scratching their heads.

"Hmm. Things are changing." An easy smile crept up on Christon's face.

Crazy good things just kept on coming. On Thursday, the defensive linebacker got really mad at practice. He threw his helmet at a teammate. That's not done. NEVER. As punishment, he wasn't allowed to play in the next game. Coach needed a replacement. He looked over the team. "Jones, you'll be starting defensive lineman for tomorrow's game."

"BOO-YAH!" Christon grabbed Pete's arm. "Can you believe it?" Then he grabbed his chest to make sure his heart didn't pound its way out. "I went from just a substitute player to the star player on the team. I got my little piece of heaven back."

The following Saturday was Game Time. Christon stood in his three-point stance. Anticipating the snap, he exploded up field, charging the opposing team's QB. He hit the QB in the hole and knocked the boogers out of him.

"Boo-yah! It's my first SACK!"

The next play, the running back got past the lineman. He was at least seven yards ahead of any player on Christon's team. Christon chased him and wrapped him up at the 40 yard line. By the end of the game, Christon managed to sack the QB three times. He got five single tackles and seven group tackles.

Pete jumped on Christon's back. "**WOW!** That was amazing. You really are a super player." Christon threw Pete off his back and put his arm over Pete's shoulder. They walked to the locker room.

"Listen up, team. Great game," said Coach. "Based on Christon's performance today, his new nickname is 'Cheetah.' And, he's now the starting defensive linebacker for the Warriors."

Christon stood frozen.

"Christon. Christon." Pete shook his good buddy. "Say something."

Christon looked at Pete. "BOO-YAH!"

GLOSSARY

3-point defensive position – bent at knees with dominant hand on ground.

Defensive End – he works to keep the opposing team from scoring; he's part of the linemen.

Fullback – the player who blocks for the running back (protects him); he also blocks to protect the quarterback.

In the hole – the space between two players.

Juke – to fake out a player, usually on the opposing team

Linemen – When the ball is in their team's possession, they run with it, attempting to score a goal; when the ball is in the opposing team's possession, they try to stop the opposing team from scoring.

QB – quarterback, he leads the team's attempts to score, usually by passing the ball to other teammates

Sack – tackle the quarterback while he still has the ball.

Safety – they're the last line of defense to keep the opposing team from scoring.

Snap – when the center throws the ball to the quarterback.

Super stiff arm – holding your arm straight out to hold off an opposing player.

Tackle – taking the ball from the opposing team's player, usually resulting in that player being knocked to the ground and losing his grip on the ball.

Wrapped him up – tackled (knocked him to the ground).

Luke, the Fullback

Joe, the Safety

Printed in the USA
CPSIA information can be obtained
at www.ICGtesting.com
LVHW060925181223
766690LV00035B/25